What risks will you take for the perfect bounty?

Mice have no business jumping in parachutes, you say?

I couldn't agree more.

And yet, here I am, about to throw myself into the void with nothing but a piece of cloth tied to my back.

But at the other end, if we succeed on this suicidal mission? The mythical Christmas cheese platter with its deliciously creamy Morbier.

Join the adventure as our hero faces his fears in his quest to put his paws on the perfect Christmas dinner.

AUTHOR OF *UNEXPECTED CONSEQUENCES*

R.W. WALLACE

Morbier Impossible

A Holiday Short Story

Morbier Impossible
by R.W. Wallace

Copyright © 2020 by R.W. Wallace

Cover by the author
Cover Illustration 115880438 © Victoria Novak | Dreamstime.com
Cover Illustration 140855497 © Sergii Syzonenko | Dreamstime.com

All characters and events in this book, other than those clearly in the public domain, are fictitious and any resemblance to real persons, living or dead, is purely coincidental.

All rights reserved. No part of this publication may be reproduced, distributed, or transmitted in any form or by any means, including photocopying, recording, or other electronic or mechanical methods, without the prior written permission of the publisher, except in the case of brief quotations embodied in critical reviews and certain other noncommercial uses permitted by copyright law. For permission requests, write to the publisher, addressed "Attention: Permissions Coordinator," at the address below.

www.rwwallace.com

ISBN: [979-10-95707-50-9]

Main category—Fiction
Other category—Fantasy

First Edition

14 13 12 11 10 / 10 9 8 7 6 5 4 3 2 1

Also by R.W. Wallace

Mystery

The Tolosa Mystery Series
The Red Brick Haze (free)
The Red Brick Cellars
The Red Brick Basilica

Ghost Detective Shorts
Just Desserts
Lost Friends
Family Bonds
Common Ground

Short Stories
Hidden Horrors
Critters
Gertrude and the Trojan Horse
First Impressions
Let Them Eat Cake
Out of Sight
Two's Company
Like Mother Like Daughter

Science Fiction (short stories)
The Vanguard
Quarantine
Common Enemies
Coiled Danger
Mars Meeting

Other short stories
Size Matters
Unexpected Consequences

Morbier Impossible

I HADN'T REALLY thought I was afraid of heights before this moment. The kitchen table never fazed me, the kitchen counter was easy play, and the top cupboards were easy peasy so long as I stayed away from the edge.

But here I am, in the rafters above the living room, my tail shaking from fear and my paws clutching nervously into the lines in the wood as Lana is explaining for the hundredth time how to work the parachute.

Yes, parachute. On a mouse.

Years ago, Bibi, one of our forefathers—I forget how many generations, I've never been good with numbers—came across a picture in the living room, one of a human falling slowly from the sky and landing safely on the ground. The man wore a helmet and goggles and a backpack for the parachute and was welcomed by his friends with open arms.

Bibi swore he would make the same thing for mice and that it would change their lives drastically.

It certainly changed *his* life; he died when he tested the first prototype.

But before moving into the afterlife of infinite cheese, Bibi passed on his passion for flying to several other mice. The crazy ones. The ones who wanted to get the humans' food from the kitchen table instead of the trash. Who thought mice should have the best parts of the cheese and not just the crust or the moldy bits. The ones who thought baiting and running away from the cat was *a game*.

Unfortunately, having no survival instinct isn't the same as being stupid and they figured out how to make it work. Only lost two more lives during flight tests.

And now, here, today, it's *me* who's supposed to fling myself into the void, with nothing but a flimsy piece of cloth to save me from splattering myself all over the tiled living room floor.

See, as it turns out, human napkins are the *perfect* size for making parachutes for mice.

Morbier Impossible

The research department nicked a whole lot of them from the humans, in different sizes and materials. The paper napkins weren't solid enough, which Huba discovered to his chagrin when he fell to the floor with a splat while the napkin gently flowed down after him, folding in on itself as it did a little dance in the air. The high quality linen napkins were too heavy and didn't hold the air well enough. Cara was more lucky than Huba in that she survived her slow-motion fall but her right hind leg would never be the same.

The cotton everyday napkins were just right. Yuba did a victory dance and was allotted an extra piece of Josephine cheese when he elegantly landed on all four legs after jumping off the old fridge in the basement. The parachute had unfolded itself perfectly, and the strings attached to the four corners of the napkin and Yuba's four legs held without a problem.

The prototype was validated.

Which is how it ended up on my back. I'm in the best team of hunters our family has seen in generations. Our team of four has pulled off the most impressive catches, going from an entire loaf of bread to two choice pieces of Roquefort blue cheese. That last one earned us our names in the hall of fame.

So it seemed natural—to everyone except me, that is—that our team should use the parachutes to pull off the heist of the decade.

See, there's one time of year that is particularly frustrating for a food-loving mouse, and that's Christmas. The humans bring in extra amounts of food this time of year, and it's meatier and fatter and sweeter than anything they eat at any other time.

This does, of course, mean that there is also more leftovers and more waste—but the mice are all too aware of the stuff they're missing out on.

There's a myth that the hunters like to tell each other on cold winter afternoons while they wait for the humans to go to bed so they can start their work. It's the story of Tutu.

Tutu *loved* duck fat. Couldn't get enough of it. Whenever the humans ate duck, Tutu would hang out in the compost for *days*, licking up every last drop of fat. Watching humans eat foie gras was pure torture for him. But nothing, and I mean *nothing*, is guarded as closely as the foie gras. It's impossible to get to and get out alive.

Tutu decided that he didn't care about that last part. He just wanted the foie gras. So on one New Year's Eve, while two humans were preparing the starters for their seven-course dinner, Tutu went hunting in the kitchen.

In broad daylight, with humans right there.

He didn't care. He was in a haze of duck fat and couldn't see farther than the slices of his favorite dish lined up next to litchis, onion jam, and toast.

Rumor has it, one of the humans saw him while he was making his way through the first slice and dropped a mouse trap on his head. The *snap* of the trap could be heard all the way down in the basement and the scream of the human was even louder.

Morbier Impossible

Most mice are able to forego the foie gras. It was Tutu's favorite but he was always a bit weird. But the thing that no mouse can ever stop lusting after?

Cheese.

And what day of the year do the humans buy an *inhuman* amount of the delicious stuff? Christmas. It comes after the salad and before the first dessert. The more people invited for dinner, the more cheese. The calculus department has tried to find an exact correlation for years but hasn't figured out the correct formula yet.

To me, knowing that a lot of humans means a lot of cheese is enough.

And this year, there are a lot of them. At least fifteen according to the last reports of the spymaster.

I'm willing to bet there will be at least ten to twelve different cheeses.

And the mice won't be able to get their paws on any of them. The cheeses always go straight from the refrigerator—which no mouse has ever managed to get into—to a large wooden serving platter that is placed on the rickety old table in the living room corner.

There's no way for a mouse to get *onto* that table. Some have managed to climb up the legs but there's no way to reach the edge of the table top—they always fall to the floor. There's no way to jump onto it from any place nearby—everything is *just* too far away.

The only way onto that table would be from above.

Hence the parachutes.

"Now, remember," Lana tells me as she shoves the end of a string into my paw. "You jump, then you pull—straight away!—and the parachute will open." She's having trouble looking me in the eye because of the helmet falling into her eyes but she doesn't seem to care.

Did you know that hazelnuts are the perfect size to make helmets for mice?

Well, the research department figured it out. Another piece of string under the chin and, *tada!*, we have helmets just like the human in the picture.

Luckily, nobody figured out how to make goggles.

My helmet is chafing on my ears and isn't far from falling into my eyes but I'm not going to take it off. I don't actually *believe* that it will protect me from anything—it's more likely to break my neck than anything else—but I'm also thinking that you never know. What if I find myself in a situation where the helmet *will* save me? So it stays on.

"This isn't going to work, Lana," I say. "That platter stays unsupervised for no more than fifteen minutes so we won't have time for more than one jump. And nobody ever figured out how to steer these things, so the chances of us actually landing *on* the table are, like… Did we not ask the calculus department to look into that? Maybe we should abort."

Morbier Impossible

Lana gives me a distracted pat on the muzzle. "Worst case scenario is all four of us landing away from the table and we'll go home empty-handed. No biggie. Now. Focus. The salad went out five minutes ago—the platter should arrive any minute. We have to get into position."

Our two teammates are on the next beam over. We've decided to spread out because neither beam is *directly* over the table and we have no idea how the parachutes will behave in such a large space.

Jumping off a human-height refrigerator and a two-story-high rafter isn't really the same thing.

Let's not think about that.

Lana sets up as far along the beam as she can get without putting herself in danger of falling off. I stop about a meter ahead of her. We wave the all-clear signal to our teammates and settle in to wait.

It doesn't take long. As there's a surge of noise from the humans at the other end of the large living room, a human with long dark hair comes in from the kitchen.

She's carrying a platter the likes of which I've never seen.

"I count fourteen cheeses," Lana says in awe. "There have *never* been that many before. Holy cheese, I'm hungry."

My mouth waters as I watch the feast approach. The human sets the platter down on the table, adjusts the angle of one of the blue cheeses, and walks back to join the rest of the group.

"All right, people," Lana yells as she signals to our mates. "We have fifteen minutes. Go! Go! Go!"

And she jumps off the wooden beam, her mouth open wide and teeth glistening, her eyes glinting with the high of the hunt.

She pulls on the string—and the parachute unfolds.

On the other beam, I see the two other hunters throw themselves into the void, one with his eyes closed and the other clutching the string in her paw so hard I can see her paw shaking from the strain from where I'm standing.

Three parachutes deployed.

Only me left.

I really, really don't want to do this.

But I can't let my team down, can't let them take all the risks without me. So I close my eyes, make sure I hold the deployment string firmly in one paw—

And I jump.

This is *nothing* like jumping off the old refrigerator.

I can feel the fact that there's nothing solid anywhere around me, just a lot of empty space, and the inevitably approaching hardwood floor. My fur is rippling around my body and the string under my chin is somehow digging into my throat as the helmet tries to act as a parachute.

I pull on the deployment string.

My entire body jerks as the parachute unfolds and my descent is abruptly slowed. Then I'm left rocking gently back and forth and I finally find the courage to open my eyes.

Morbier Impossible

Across the room, the humans around their feast, none of them looking in our direction. Below me, the platter of cheese, already a lot closer than before.

And on my right, a door slamming open.

A gust of cold air sweeps across the room, making several of the humans yell their displeasure at the tall short-haired human coming through the door.

I rock a little under my parachute but nothing too worrisome.

My teammates, however, are not so fortunate.

They take the brunt of the blast from the door. Lana is flung against the wall, her helmet making a dull *clonk* on impact. The parachute deflates partially but it still slows her descent along the wall down to the floor.

She hits the hardwood with a soft squeak.

Nunu is not so fortunate. The gust of wind makes her do several spins around the parachute—up and down at least three times—and when she hits the wall, the parachute deflates completely, making her free-fall from at least as high as the refrigerator in the basement.

She doesn't make a sound. I'm worried.

My last teammate, Enzo, was far enough from the wall to avoid hitting it but he's thrown way off course. He's not going to land on the table.

The door closes and everything calms down. As far as I can tell, none of the humans have seen the four mice parachuting down on their cheese platter.

I wasn't thrown off course at all by that gust of wind. Quite the contrary, actually.

Moments later, I land lightly smack in the middle of the cheese platter, right on top of the Camembert. A frisson runs up my legs as I feel the soft fur covering the crust under my paws.

I've landed in paradise.

I scramble to unfasten the parachute and as the adrenaline of the flight tapers off, I hear squeaks.

I recognize Lana and her favorite swear words when something goes sideways. And someone's screaming in pain. I can't tell if it's Enzo or Nunu but remembering their descents, it's probably Nunu.

At least she's not dead.

I extricate myself from the strings, jump off the Camembert, and run to the edge of the table to check on my friends.

Enzo has only just landed and is working on freeing himself but is having issues with one of his rear legs.

Nunu is lying by the wall, her parachute still attached and useless, and her small, furry body writhing in pain. Lana reaches her, her parachute still attached to one leg and trailing behind her.

I need to get down there and help them with Nunu.

"Don't you dare come down here without any cheese!" Lana yells at me. "We're taking care of Nunu—you get the food!"

"But…" I shake myself, trying to focus.

The food.

Morbier Impossible

We came here, and took a lot of really big risks, just so we could put our paws on that delicious cheese. Now, here I am, on the fabled cheese platter, but my friend is on the floor in agony.

"We've got her covered," Enzo yells. He has joined the two others and is rapidly untying the parachute strings from Nunu's legs. "*Get the cheese!*"

Fine. I'll get the cheese.

I scramble back to the platter.

There's so much to choose from. Where do I even start?

The large Tomme is out of the question. Even if there had been four of us, we wouldn't have been able to move it. The Roquefort is so mature it's already crumbling. I can get some of it with me but only as much as I can carry in my paws—so hardly any.

There's a Morbier—aw, man, a Morbier—my *favorite* ever cheese. It's creamy and mellow and softer than butter. Its identifying streak of ashes gives it that little extra touch that I just can't resist.

Really, I can't resist.

I run over and nip one tiny piece and gobble it right down.

Then back to work. As much as I love the Morbier, I won't be able to push it off the table all by myself, nor will we be able to get it out of sight before the humans return.

The humans!

I scramble off the platter. There were supposed to be four of us; three for stealing the cheese and one for keeping a lookout. How am I supposed to do everything all on my own?

The humans are still at the table. Some are still eating but for the most part, they're sitting a short distance back from the table, leaning back against the backrests of their chairs, leaving room for their bulging bellies.

My resolve strengthens. I will also have a bulging belly by the end of the night, just you wait and see.

I have to pick a target. As I sprint across the platter several times, I just can't find one that's small enough for me to manage on my own.

Until I hit the goat cheese.

It's *just* the right size. A disk that's maybe a centimeter thick and a little less than my own size across. It's quite light, so I should be able to lift it up on its edge.

I test my theory and find that, yes, I can lift it, then scurry over to the edge of the table to check on my friends.

They've made a stretcher of one of the parachutes and put Nunu inside. Enzo has looped several of the strings over his shoulders and as I watch, he pulls forward while Lana pushes from the back—and the stretcher inches forward.

"Hey, guys!" I yell down at them. "I think I can get a goat cheese. What's the plan?"

Morbier Impossible

Lana looks up at me while pushing. "We have to get Nunu to safety first, but I'll be back to help you repatriate the cheese. Just get it off the table while we're gone!"

The stretcher moves a little faster now and they're aiming straight for the entrance to our lair behind the living room buffet. I scan the room to make sure the coast is clear—

"The cat's coming!"

The panic makes my voice squeak even higher than usual. Nunu would have made fun of me if she wasn't writhing in pain on that stretcher down there.

The cat—that awful, ginormous, diabolical russet-and-brown beast—is standing in the cat door leading to the garage, his blue eyes sharp and his whiskers twitching.

My teammates see him too. None of us dare say another word because the monster's hearing is out of this world. They do speed up, though, pulling and pushing the parachute stretcher across the floor as fast as it will go.

Unless I want to jump down from the table and abandon the cheese, there's nothing I can do to help my friends right now, so although my instincts are telling me to *run! run!*, I scramble back to the goat cheese and get to work.

I push it up on its edge and start rolling it off the platter. It's so simple that I'm wondering if I should attempt a second one.

The cat streaking across the room stops that thought short.

He has spotted the fleeing mice.

And they're so close to safety, too.

Enzo is pulling with all his might, his helmet abandoned halfway across the hardwood floor. Lana's legs are moving so fast, she doesn't get a real grip on the wood and ends up spinning in place.

The cat is already over halfway there.

They're not going to make it.

I scream out the loudest squeak I can.

The cat stops in his tracks, his ears turned toward me.

Clearly having lost all common sense, I stand up on my haunches and wave at him. "Why don't you try to catch me, you great lout? I'm the one stealing the cheese, after all."

On that thought, I give the goat cheese a last push and it goes over the edge.

It lands with a soft splat—it's possible I won't be able to roll it away on the floor as easily as I had across the table.

Then my mind turns to survival, because the cat has accepted my challenge.

He's leaping toward me, murder in his eyes.

I'm about to jump off the table when I see the humans moving. Someone has seen the cat streaking across the room and is wondering what's happening.

If they see a mouse running across the floor, they're certainly not going to be opposed to the cat "doing his job." They'll probably help him do the deed.

If they don't know I'm here, though…

Morbier Impossible

I scramble back to the cheese platter. If I remember correctly…yes! Right there.

The Crottin du Cocumont. Somebody has already cut out a slice. There's room for me to hide. The crust is even the same color as my gray fur so if I'm lucky, it might seem like there's just one big slab of soot-crusted cheese, and no mouse.

I scurry into the V-shaped cut in the cheese just as the cat jumps up on the table and one of the humans shouts out.

I do my best not to move.

At first, the difficulty comes from not shaking with fear. But as my nose realizes where it is, my brain short-circuits.

I'm surrounded by cheese on all sides. It's soft and porous and juicy and just…perfection.

Honestly, if I have to die today, it might as well be here.

I'm starting to understand Tutu and his foie gras.

Careful not to move the rest of my body, I try to cock my head to nip a piece of cheese—but I'm blocked by the helmet. The stupid, ridiculous hazelnut helmet that they made us wear.

Then I'm ripped back to the present as the entire platter is shaken by the cat's arrival.

"Oh no, you don't!" It's one of the humans who live here. Could my plan be working?

"Shoo! Get off the table! That cheese is not for you, you've got your Christmas dinner in the kitchen. Shoo!"

Lifting my head slightly, I catch a glimpse of the human forcibly lifting the cat off the table, his claws out and his eyes crazy. I'm tempted to wave again but this time I refrain.

"I guess it's time for the cheese," the human says from the kitchen door once she's gotten rid of the cat. "You guys ready?"

Oh no. Being on *this* table is risky enough but if I find myself on the *main* table, where there are over a dozen humans—I'm toast.

I've never moved so fast in my life.

I scramble out of the Crottin and toward the table edge, so much in a hurry that I don't notice one of my hind legs getting caught in the string of my parachute until I'm tumbling over the edge with the thing still attached.

"Oh, good, you thought to remove the evidence." Lana is back and she's all business.

While I try to recover from my fall—fine, I'll admit the helmet finally came in handy—she grabs the parachute and folds it over the goat cheese that's standing just a few paces off. It's now more half-moon shaped than full moon but it's still an entire goat cheese.

"Come on!" she yells at me and starts across the floor with the strings over her shoulders.

I scramble after her and push our bounty ahead of me as we scurry for cover.

"Are those two *mice* pushing a napkin across the floor? Are they wearing *helmets*?"

Morbier Impossible

I almost freeze in fear as I hear the human voice but Lana urges me to keep pushing.

"Don't be daft, Didier. How much have you had to drink?"

"This is only my second glass!"

"Second glass of red. There was the white before that, and the Muscat for the starters…"

The laughter and voices fade away as we push through the hole under the buffet.

We made it.

That night, our names go on the wall of fame for the second time.

It's the first time in recorded history—I checked with the historians—that anyone has brought back *an entire cheese*.

It's only slightly dented and fully delicious and the entire family thanks us as they get a taste.

I've put my helmet up in a niche in the wall and Lana decorated it with some chocolate wrapper she found by the kitchen sink. It looks kind of like the decorations the humans set up for Christmas.

And this year, we also got our feast.

tHANK YOU

THANK YOU FOR reading *Morbier Impossible*. I hope you enjoyed it. And feel free to tell others about it if you did!

If you liked the the story, you might want to check out some of my other books mentioned on the next page. It's mostly Mysteries, but a few other genre short stories will pop up, too.

And don't forget that the first book of my *Tolosa Mystery* series, *The Red Brick Haze*, is available for free on my website.

R.W. Wallace
www.rwwallace.com

About the Author

R.W. WALLACE WRITES in most genres, though she tends to end up in mystery more often than not. Dead bodies keep popping up all over the place whenever she sits down in front of her keyboard.

The stories mostly take place in Norway or France; the country she was born in and the one that has been her home for two decades. Don't ask her why she writes in English—she won't have a sensible answer for you.

Her Ghost Detective short story series appears in *Pulphouse Magazine*, starting in issue #9.

You can find all her books, long and short, all genres, on rwwallace.com.

Also by R.W. Wallace

Mystery

The Tolosa Mystery Series
The Red Brick Haze (free)
The Red Brick Cellars
The Red Brick Basilica

Ghost Detective Shorts (coming soon)
Just Desserts
Lost Friends
Family Bonds
Till Death
Family History
Common Ground
Heritage
Eternal Bond
New Beginnings

Short Stories
Cold Blue Eternity
Hidden Horrors
Critters
Gertrude and the Trojan Horse
First Impressions
Let Them Eat Cake
Out of Sight
Two's Company
Like Mother Like Daughter

FANTASY (SHORT STORIES)
Unexpected Consequences
Morbier Impossible
A Second Chance

SCIENCE FICTION (SHORT STORIES)
The Vanguard

LOLLAPALOOZA SHORTS
Quarantine
Common Enemies
Coiled Danger
Mars Meeting

ADVENTURE (SHORT STORIES)
Size Matters

www.ingramcontent.com/pod-product-compliance
Lightning Source LLC
LaVergne TN
LVHW051923060526
838201LV00060B/4160